BRUNO
AND THE
NEW PLANE

Let's just see now...
I think I know how.

Colin and Jacqui Hawkins

ORCHARD BOOKS

To the irrepressible Brough, and
for Gail for putting up with him!
Love, Colin and Jacqui

ORCHARD BOOKS, 96 Leonard Street, London EC2A 4XD
Orchard Books Australia, 32/45-51 Huntley Street, Alexandria, NSW 2015
www.wattspublishing.co.uk
ISBN 1 84362 259 9 (hardback)
ISBN 1 84362 412 5 (paperback)
First published in Great Britain in 1989
This edition published in hardback 2003 and paperback 2004
Text and illustrations © Colin and Jacqui Hawkins 2003
(hardback) 10 9 8 7 6 5 4 3 2 1
(paperback) 10 9 8 7 6 5 4 3 2 1
Printed in Hong Kong, China

Bruno Bear loved making things.
One day, he set off to build
something very special.

I know what to make, but how long will it take?

Do not disturb

BANG!

BASH!

Is it a bird?

Don't be absurd!

All morning, loud noises came
from Bruno's workshop.

After a long, long time…out came Bruno,
proudly pushing a brand-new plane.
He said,

I think I might go for a flight.

SQUEAK

Bruno's pals all rushed round to see
his new shiny plane and they said,

Bruno thought that they might like to try out the plane with him.

But suddenly, everyone was extremely busy.
No one wanted to fly. They all made their excuses.

Bruno wondered what was wrong.
What could be more fun than flying?

So Bruno decided to go on his own.
He scrambled into the little cockpit and said,

Perhaps his pals would join him later.

Let's have a look.
It's all in this book.

One, two.
Here's what
you do.

Three, four.
Engines roar.

Five, six.
Pull on joystick.

Seven, eight.
I can hardly
wait!

Nine, ten.
Let's go then!

With a mighty roar, the little red plane
leapt into the air as Bruno Bear shouted,

Ready, steady, GO!

ROAR

Bruno looped and swooped through the air. Round and round the sky he flew. It was so easy-peasy!

Bruno had spotted his friend Charlie Crocodile fishing from old Humpy Bridge.

So, Bruno swung his new plane around and zoomed down towards Charlie who said,

The plane caught Charlie's fishing line. But Charlie hung on and reeled himself aboard.

Bruno flew his new plane on, over Ronnie, Ellie and Paddy having a picnic. Charlie saw them and said,

Ronnie, Ellie and Paddy squealed in fright
as the plane scooped them off the ground.

The little plane soared up into the air, with the tent in tow. They all clambered aboard and said,

Everyone clung on tight as Bruno flew higher and higher and higher.

Suddenly...

...the engine stopped!

And down they plunged
towards the ground.

The shiny new plane hurtled towards Holly,
hanging out her washing. Everyone shouted,

Holly and her clean washing
were catapulted skywards. Then...

Bruno's new plane and all his pals crashed nose-first into a gigantic tree.

Then everything went very quiet. The dazed friends gazed at Bruno in amazement as he giggled and said,

Bruno helped everyone scramble down from
the tree and they all set off for home.

On foot!